NOW I AM FIVE!

by Jane Belk Moncure

illustrated by Helen Endres

created by THE CHILD'S WORLD

 CHILDRENS PRESS, CHICAGO

Library of Congress Cataloging in Publication Data

Moncure, Jane Belk.

Now I am five.
Summary: A child displays the many achievements of a
five-year-old.
[1. Growth—Fiction]   I. Endres, Helen, ill.
II. Title.
PZ7.M739Nof   1984   [E]   83-25264
ISBN 0-516-01879-5

NOW I AM FIVE!

Now that I'm five,
I can jump very
high. . .

when an ocean
wave comes
splashing by.

I can build castles
in the sand. . .

and count the seashells
in my hand.

Now that I'm five,

I can skip when we hike.

I can put on my
roller skates. . .

ride a bike.

Now that I'm five,
I help Mama bake
by stirring the batter. . .

and icing the cake.

I can help wash
the dishes. . .

help make up my
bed. . .

take care of my
kitten. . .

and see that she's
fed.

I can print my name. . .

cut and "sew". . .

polish my shoes. . .
tie a bow.

And now that I'm five, guess where I go.

I go to kindergarten!
My friends go too!

There are so many fun things to do!

We have
picture books. . .

paints. . .

24

puzzles. . .

and clay.

We have puppets,
a playhouse and. . .

games to play.

We have music
and dancing. . .

storytime too.

Best of all is our
trip to the petting
zoo.

I'm glad that I'm five! There is so much to do.
Tell me, do you like to be five too?